<u>How To Catch A Demon</u>

A Baseline for the Christian

Theological Perspective on Demonic

Possession

By Stephen Hancock

September 2020

ISBN: 9798683450915

Table of Contents

Prologue

Not so many days ago, I found myself listening to a podcast. The topic, like it so often is, was on apologetics. Those involved were going through many of the common atheistic or anti-theistic arguments and providing their most common responses, rationales, and reasonings.

Most of these I had heard a million times before, until one question was brought up. It was not technically a standard apologetics question. It was not about the validity of God or Jesus, the death or resurrection, or any other topic typically considered in the world of standardized apologetics.

The question was about demons, more specifically, demonic possession as is written about in the Holy Bible. This falls under the typical "challenge to miracles" argument, an attempt to invalidate the word of God. If the bible is wholly true, then explain how it is people are writing that they cast demonic spirits or literal demons out of people. The atheist looks at this type of writing and laughs, the concept of a fabled creature such as a demon seeming to fit along nicely with their idea of the flying spaghetti monster that we call God.

More shocking than the question, the response was, "I'm not really sure."

"These individuals have Ph.D.'s," I thought to myself. How could they not be fully versed on this idea? The man speaking responded it was simply not an area that he was well versed in, and they even questioned why it was that more theological works had not been dedicated to the topic; as if it were some taboo topic within the realm of Christianity that scholars simply wished to avoid.

And so, goes the purpose of this book. Unfortunately, this topic is not narrow in scope. I prefer to write things which are quick, arrive at the point, and then be done with it. This is not an option with such a topic, as the topic itself spans centuries, different religions, and cultures, and is even subject to major variability within the same religions or cultures.

People have long been as fascinated with the idea of demons as they have been with the idea of angels.

There has been countless books, movies, and other entertainment created that focuses on the concept of demons, demonic possession, and demonology. However, very few have tried to address the actual theological position of the protestant Christian church regarding the topic.

Well, bear with me if you will. We will get to that point, but there is a lot of ground to cover before we get there.

The History of Demons

We have to start by acknowledging that Christianity (or Judaism) may not have been the first to conceptualize the notion of demons or demonic spirits. This does not in and of itself affect validity of the existence, it simply means others thought or experienced the same thing earlier, maybe.

There seems to certainly be at least some evidence that the conceptualization of demon or evil spirits pre-dates Judaism by up to 1,000 years (perhaps much longer). Of course, when we start dealing with the dating of things, people, and ideas; there is always seemingly room for argumentation.

Based on the archaeological works, specifically of Jeremy Black and Anthony Green in the early 1990's, there is quite a bit of evidence that suggests at least a conceptualization of a demon amongst ancient Sumerians, Babylonians, and Assyrians. Most of the people of these ancient cultures had some theory or idea of an "underworld" and the evil demon spirits that resided there, some of which were given the power to come to earth to torture mortals.

The actual term "demon" did not exist at this time. The ancient

Sumerians (as an example) simply referred to the spirits as the "offspring of the underworld." They had several different words for the underworld and many different underworlds, so the "demon" was simply referred to as the offspring of whichever particular underworld.

Another interesting concept unique to these demons were that they were not necessarily totally malevolent in nature. Many were good or were at least capable of committing positive actions. It could be argued that these specifics demons were not necessarily equivalent to the monotheistic religions demons which would arise soon enough. It could very well be argued that these demons resembled more of a hybrid combination of angels and demons.

Very similarly to other mythologically inspired ancient cultures, these underworld offspring seemed to serve explanatory purposes. Mesopotamia's Lamashtu for instance, an ancient demonic spirit or goddess, was claimed to have fed on infant blood and if the infant were not dead, would cause deformities. This was used to help explain why miscarriages and birth deformities occurred, since obviously given the time period there was no other understood explanation.

Attempting to evaluate the timelines that existed is quite a challenge. Some archaeologists like to say the introduction of these demonic type spirits into cultures appeared as far back as 3000 BC. However, the overwhelming majority of the evidence for this introduction appears to take place between 2300-2000 BC.

Oddly, it may be to some extent argued that the idea (or more appropriately the explanation) of demonic spirits occurs simultaneously across cultures, at least in written form. It is not well understood just how far back the concept of demonic spirits exist in Hinduism and other Asian tribalized religions. This is because prior to around 1,500 BC (rise of the Indus Valley Civilization), the traditional version of Hinduism did not exist. There was numerous tribal forms of the religion with a variety of different beliefs and worship practices that arguably date back far before that of the ancient Sumerians. Some of which had demonic spirit like characters and some that did not.

If we attribute modern archaeology standards to Judaism, Judaism essentially claims that there has always been evil or demonic spirits. The Book of

Genesis quickly begins with talking about essentially the evil spirit (serpent) that tempted Eve. With some assumption made toward the deep oral tradition of the ancient Israelites/Canaanites, we could likely extrapolate that they proposed their own demon or evil spirit concept dating back to around 2000 BC as well. Again, prior to this, when the differing nomadic tribes were splintered, there could likely have been many that subscribed to the idea already.

My personal postulation is that the concept of evil or demonic spirits exist equally as far back as any concept of God or an afterlife. This is because many ancient cultures passed ideas along exclusively via oral history. The concept of written documentation of beliefs and history is a much more modern invention on the human timeline.

It is important to note a uniqueness to the Judeo-Christian initial conceptualization of an evil spirit. In all of the other examples from and prior to the era, the evil spirits serve very specific purposes. Whether it was to explain bad weather, death, famine, or any other tragedy of the time, these other spirits always functioned as an explanation for something otherwise not understood. But they were always explaining naturalistic events, physical events taking place in the real world at the time.

The Judeo-Christian version spins this idea slightly. The evil spirit incarnated through the serpent (many scholars would say Satan), is used to explain the psychology of humans themselves. It is still serving an explanatory function, but not necessarily a naturalistic function. This approach actually attempts to follow logical observation in a way that the others do not. This kind of rationalization and use of logical thinking is quite impressive considering it was thought of by essentially a poorly educated primarily nomadic tribe.

They clearly were concerned with the idea that humans were highly capable of committing evil acts. Instead of wondering about why it is women have miscarriages, they sought to find why it was that one human could behave so atrociously toward another human, even in the absence of an obvious motivator for such behavior.

It could be argued (to view this non-religiously) that they employed a type of archetypal logic to the nature of humanity. If God represented the ultimate good, then there must equally be something that represented the ultimate bad (it is not in practice this purely dualistic). If God is the archetype for all goodness, then the conceptualization of "Satan" or whatever possessed that snake, as an archetype for all evil follows a certain level of reason. The origin of the Judeo-Christian demon is not something that kills babies or causes disease, it is the spirit that pushes and divides humans away from God.

Old Testament Goats

With a little background behind us, we can begin to start to evaluate what is actually written about demons and demonic spirits in the bible itself. This of course begins with a look at the old testament.

For cultural context, the word demon itself as currently understood did not exist throughout most of the old testament writings. The ancient Greek word "Daemon" originally simply meant a divine spirit or divine power and traditionally had a positive connotation not a negative one. In his writings Plato described Socrates as being "daemon," extolling high praise on Socrates... not accusing him of being what we would think of as demonic.

For this etymological reason, there is not a direct translatory word for demon in the Hebrew language. The common word found for demon in the old testament is *Shedim* which most directly translates to a mythological evil spirit or someone having an evil disposition. We will come back to this shortly.

Some may get distracted now by the existence of the word "Satan" in the old testament. We will address it now, if not, it will be the elephant in the room so to speak. Many have the opinion that the word "Satan" as used commonly, had the same meaning in original Hebrew text as it currently does today, being synonymous with the word's "devil" or "lucifer." This is, at least partially, inaccurate.

Let's begin with Adam and Eve, it should be noted that nothing in the story of the Garden of Eden references demons, Satan, or anything else along those lines. The translation is literally a snake or serpent. Now could this be a metaphor, certainly, but we play a dangerous game with this story in assuming that certain elements are metaphorical or symbolic and that other elements are not. Or more appropriately, we should avoid making assumptions. Though something certainly possessed the snake, nowhere does it state that Satan the being was the possessor.

The word "Satan" appears ten times in the old testament. The direct definition of these uses is "the adversary" or "the accuser" and in traditional Judaism this always represents a "human adversary (or accuser)."

Some quick examples of this type of use:

1 Chronicles 21:1 in the King James Version states, "Satan stood up against Israel." However, the

literal translation of this verse is, "And there standeth up an adversary against Israel."

We can see here that the reference is not to a literal "demon" but a real-world human adversary. Some Christian scholars might argue that this verse infers David was being tempted literally by Satan. However, it is worth pointing out the traditional rabbinic scholars and many Christian scholars would argue that the adversary David was facing was his own pride, not the literal influence of the devil himself.

Psalm 109:6 likewise in the King James Version states, "Set Thou a wicked man over him, and let Satan stand at his right hand."

But the literal translation of this verse is, "Appoint Thou over him the wicked, And an adversary standeth at his right hand."

This verse and chapter provides a very direct explanation of the term Satan. The context that follows this verse directly references someone "being accused" not someone being influenced by Satan. This translational difference covers the ten verses using the original word "Satan."

But there is a problem. Job. The Book of Job throws a huge

monkey wrench into this whole thing.

Between the Book of Job and the Book of Zechariah there is an additional 13 uses of the word *Satan* only this time the word used is *Ha-Satan* not just *Satan*.

We run into an issue with this translation because in Job, Satan responds to God with words, indicating some type of literal being. I mean, they have a conversation, right?

Here the existence of *Ha-Satan* causes quite the odd theological problem. Traditional Judaism often views this problem irrelevantly, some Jewish scholars go so far as to claim Job is not an actual event to be taken literally, simply a story or poem meant to convey a powerful message. This is not a Christian perspective as it amounts to little more than picking and choosing which parts of the Bible you wish to believe are to be taken literally or not.

But parsing through the *Satan* of Job is no easy task, take for instance that the Book of Job is one of the only biblical books that John Calvin refused to write a commentary on. The whole concept of Satan as a literal entity is even debated among modern Christians. How do we tackle the issue of demons when we cannot even agree on the issue of Satan? Can we have demonic spirits without Satan?

An increasing number of Christians hold the Judaist view that Satan is not an entity but simply a representation of human evils. This is a highly biologically driven view of human evil that has taken off in the post-enlightenment liberal theological world. The notion is simply that all humans via the animalistic portions of their brain are hardwired for evil, only through a search for God and following his commands do we overcome this base instinctual drive. Many famous psychiatrist including

Sigmund Freud posited similar explanations for the idea of Satan.

Christians, and seemingly Jews as well, run afoul with this claim. There is no way to reconcile this interpretation of Satan with the Bible thanks to Job (as well as the entire new testament, i.e. when Satan tempts Jesus). We either have to call into question Job, ignore Job, or we have to call into question Satan; all of which leave us with the end result that the bible is flawed and certainly not infallible. Satan is simply too important of a figure, especially once we enter the new testament, to use this type of thinking.

A famous quote from a story told by the late Dr. R.C. Sproul: he asked his class "How can you all believe in a supernatural force for good (God) yet equally *not* believe in a supernatural force for evil (Satan)?" As many theologians have expressed, the greatest deceit that Satan ever committed was convincing everyone he doesn't even exist.

The Christian theology has to be that Satan as an independent being exist, as Biola University Professor J. Warner stated, "a personal, evil, subordinate being." Does this mean that all evil occurs directly from such a being's influence? Theoretically yes, if we consider the ideas of original sin, but I would say in reality no.

Someone for instance might have an affair. It is not necessary for an evil entity to exist for this to occur. There is a biological impulse which will lead to this behavior all on their own (though the argument could be made if such good and evil entities did not exist would the action be objectively wrong or evil to begin with?).

However, if we take for instance the actions of Hitler, or perhaps something more recent like the mass shooting in Las Vegas, Nevada; we run in to quite the quandary in trying to chalk it all up to biological impulse or even mental health problems. There is clearly something not easily quantified acting on a person's being that pushes them to this point, it would be a grave simplification to just claim environmental forces over time in an attempt to make a failing psychological explanation.

It is sufficient enough at this point doctrinally to state that an actual being exists in some capacity as the catalyst for evil. I do not think it is the Christian's place to espouse to what degree, force, or will this entity is allowed to act with. The Christian principle would simply be that this Satan is ultimately subordinate to God, exist, and the mission is to separate the person from the creator. It should be noted this doctrinal view of Satan is highly limiting, God does not allow Satan to force us to sin against our own will, we are given the freedom and the power to simply push back against these temptations. James 4:7 "So humble yourselves before God. Resist the devil, and he will flee from you." However, for the non-believer it could be said that Satan is given far more power and influence.

Though slightly sidetracked, this will be all that is covered on Satan specifically. It is necessary, to even cover the demon topic, to accept Satan as essentially the ruler of all demons. As we see in Matthew 12:24, "But when the Pharisees heard this, they said, "It is only by Beelzebul, the prince of demons, that this fellow drives out demons." Again, off topic, this verse infers that ancient Jewish priest had a far different view of Satan than modern Judaism which appears to outright reject it.

Now back to the idea and concept of demons in the old testament.

Many well-respected Christian scholars hold to the belief that the commonly known idea of "demons" is found throughout the old the testament.

Though I clearly disagree with many Jewish scholars concerning the Satan issue, I tend to agree with them in reference to the meaning of demons as it occurs in the old testament.... That mostly being that it does not actually seem to exist in the old testament, or if does exist it used to serve literary purposes. (Remember, we are talking about demons now, not Satan)

Demons are referenced frequently throughout the old testament in modern translation, but we have to remember the word demon at the time in Greek writing had generally positive connotations and there was not a direct translation from ancient Hebrew to mean what we currently know as *demon*.

The main use of demon appears in instances such as Deuteronomy 32:17, "They sacrificed unto devils (demons in some translations), not to God; to gods whom they knew not, to new gods that came newly up, whom your fathers feared not."

In the context of human and animal sacrifice throughout the old testament, there is the repetitive use of this form of the Hebrew word *Shedim*. This is the most common form used in the old testament and is found in all the verses contextualized with some form of false sacrifice (i.e. Psalm 106:37).

The more literal translation is *false god* not demon or devil. The sacrifices taking place were to false gods, the word being used was simply translated to demon or devil.

Other old testament verses, still centered around the concept of sacrifice, use the Hebrew word *Se'Irim*. This word roughly comes from the Hebrew word *Sa'Ir*. Or the word we would most know it as *Satyr*. Literally, a half-man, half-goat. Leviticus 17:7 provides an example of this use.

"And they shall no more offer their sacrifices unto devils, after whom they have gone a whoring. This shall be a statute forever unto them throughout their generations."

The word devils here is *Se'Irim*. Again, this is basically saying they are sacrificing to a false god, but this use is especially contemptuous. They are essentially calling the other god something the equivalent of a horned-man demon-goat. It is the modern equivalent of trash talk.

With these examples aside, there is specific demons that are mentioned in the old testament, but we do not find them possessing people. Instead, these demons are essentially indentured to the service of God.

An example of this is the demon Dever. This is found in Habakkuk 3:5 and Psalms 91:6 amongst other places.

Habakkuk 3:5 "Plague went before him; pestilence followed his steps."

Psalms 91:6 "Nor for the pestilence that walketh in darkness; nor for the destruction that wasteth at noonday."

Interestingly the original Hebrew word used here for pestilence is *Dever*. This word, especially among Jewish scholars, is thought to have been used intentionally, as *Dever* was well-known across multiple regions and religions as the "demon of pestilence." Even more odd, in the Habakkuk verse the word for *plague* is *Resheph*. The ancient Canaanites as well as far East religions would have recognized this as a reference to the "god (or demon) of the plague."

The Habakkuk verse is essentially talking about these two *demons* who are proceeding God (YHWH) into the great battle. For this reason, there is clearly an issue on whether these forces were actually "demonic" or not. It could just as easily be argued that these were angelic forces serving God's will. Either way, it is tough to view them as our modern view of demons, and we certainly have not reached a point where these spirits are possessing people.

There is several other, what would be considered at the time perhaps, popularized demons or evil spirits mentioned in the old testament; apparently used to make the writing more relatable or understandable to the reader in that time.

In Isaiah 34:14 we find reference to the Sumerian demon Lilith, an evil succubus who stole children and was often referenced to as a screeching-owl or night-owl.

"And met have Ziim with Aiim, And the goat for its companion calleth, Only there rested hath the *night-owl* (Lilith), And hath found for herself a place of rest. (Literal translation)"

In Jeremiah 9:21 we read, "For death hath come up into our windows, It hath come into our palaces, To cut off the suckling from without, Young men from the broad places."

This use of *death* is found also in Hosea, Job, and Isaiah. The word used for death in Hebrew being *Mavet* or *Mawet*. This would have been understood by those knowledgeable of ancient Canaanite gods to be *Mot*, the god/demon of death.

We see that the demon concept is portrayed generally in one of two ways in the old testament.

There is use of it to represent a false god being sacrificed to. There is also the referencing of specific demons from other cultures, ancient cultures, and other religions.

Into the Unknown

Now we can finally move into the more debated topic of actual demonic possession. But before we do that, we have to understand what the most common, and in my opinion, most reasonable objection is to the issue of demonic possession in the bible.

The objection is that demonic possession in the bible is equally as explanatory in nature as all the other "demons" found in ancient literature. What is it explaining exactly? Mental illness and disease.

In 1988 while writing for George Fox University, Roger Bufford identified the common elements found in all the biblical accounts of demonic possession. These are essentially the characteristics of demonic possession.

The list of characteristics is as follows:

1. Demonstrates supernatural knowledge
2. Demonstrate supernatural physical strength
3. Acts of magic
4. Bring about physical illness
5. Different voices
6. Abnormal behaviors
7. Aggressive or violent behavior
8. Distinctive personality differences

If you have ever known someone with mental illness, you immediately recognize some of these as being commonplace in those who suffer from it.

In those with Dissociative Personality Disorder (or Multiple Personality Disorder), symptoms include different voices and distinct separate personalities. Those with schizophrenia can also often times represent different personalities.

People experiencing mania or excited delirium, often via having bi-polar episodes, can seem unexpectedly strong. In the world of the unbeliever, every account of demonic possession either should or is explainable via mental illness.

This theory is preferred because it ultimately provides a biological solution to a problem represented as being supernatural.

The tact typically taken in this argument is that at the time no one understood that something such as mental disease could exist. There is some evidence that they were aware of certain emotional problems that we would equate with anxiety or depression. Often the stories of Elijah and Jonah are cited as examples of this. In Jonah 4 he exclaims multiple times how he wishes he could just die, and then goes off by himself and essentially pouts and wallows in his own seeming misfortune.

Though it appears they were aware of these different types of emotional swings, they certainly did not consider them to be the result of uncontrollable biological forces.

As a matter of fact, in stories where God encounters this type of behavior such as in Jonah, God basically shows no sympathy. As illustrated by God placing the tree to give Jonah shade from the sun, only to immediately destroy it.

In terms of more modernized disease concepts such as Dissociative Disorder and Schizophrenia, it is fair to assume the people of that time had absolutely no clue what these things were by modern standards. From there, the unbelieving can more easily make the claim that these *demons* are little more than explanations for things that the people did not understand.

From an apologetical defense standpoint, whether the person claims it was *demons* or simply mental health is irrelevant and it still falls under the umbrella of "miracles." Even if it was arguably nothing more than mental illness, the idea that Jesus or anyone else could rid someone of such an illness with little more than some words or a prayer, or even just a light touch, does not diminish the miraculous nature of the act itself.

We are still left, regardless of cause, with defending the ability to perform miraculous works... which is not what this book is geared toward.

As we push onward into the actual accounts of demonic possession, we will go back to this concept of mental illness and see if it is adequate to provide an explanation of what was occurring within the account.

Names that end in -AUL for 200

Outside of the four gospels, there is legitimately only three accounts of demonic possession to consider. One in the old testament and two in the new testament. The old testament account involves Saul. The new testament accounts revolve around Paul. Recall, we are focusing on *demons* and *demonic possession*, this is not focused or meant to include anything directly mentioned about Satan.

We start by looking at the old testament account of Saul. Here is the verses both from the King James Version and Young's Literal Translation respectively:

1 Samuel 16:14-16

"But the Spirit of the LORD
departed from Saul, and an evil
spirit from the LORD troubled him.
And Saul's servants said unto him,
Behold now, an evil spirit from God
troubleth thee. Let our lord now
command thy servants, *which
are* before thee, to seek out a
man, *who is* a cunning player on
an harp: and it shall come to pass,
when the evil spirit from God is
upon thee, that he shall play with
his hand, and thou shalt be
well.(KJV)"

"And the Spirit of Jehovah turned
aside from Saul, and a spirit of
sadness from Jehovah terrified
him; and the servants of Saul say

unto him, 'Lo, we pray thee, a spirit of sadness from God is terrifying thee; let our lord command, we pray thee, thy servants before thee, they seek a skillful man, playing on a harp, and it hath come to pass, in the spirit of sadness from God being upon thee, that he hath played with his hand, and it is well with thee.'(YLT)"

There is no consensus amongst scholars as whether or not Saul's experience represents true demonic possession. Traditional conservative commentaries such as those by Matthew Henry and John Gill ascribe to a demonic influence existing within Saul. However, both these commentators as well others rely on the earlier works of Josephus to arrive at their conclusions.

Others such as Ellicott's Commentary, the Pulpit Commentary, and the Cambridge Study Bible are not so definitive in their statements regarding the events of Saul.

Upon personal evaluation, I do not see this as a legitimate representation of demonic possession. Though the Cambridge commentary certainly states they believe it to be demonic possession, they still interestingly begin their commentary of the verses with "the cause of Saul's mental disorder."

A general consensus here is that God simply withdrew his spirit or grace away from Saul, leaving Saul to his own devices so to speak. At which point, in the absence of God's grace, Saul becomes "saddened." There is a clear psychological link here between the ideas of paranoia and depression that do not require a supernatural explanation nor is one clearly implored upon the reader. If a person were this close to God, only to find themselves in God's absence suddenly, it seems reasonable that depression would enter into anyone. Or imagine it this way; two people have a very close intimate relationship. One of them suddenly leaves the other with little prior warning. The other person becomes depressed and distrusting. This is a common human experience. We typically do not claim that the now depressed person is possessed demonically, however we might say that their spirit has now been broken or exist in tumult over the events.

There is a significant number of biblical parallels here: Psalm 81:12, several verses in Romans 1, Isaiah 30:1, and Acts 14:16 just to a name of few. In these verses we equally find the withdrawal of God leading to great tragedy or general misery for the individual, group, or nation. They were not all possessed by demonic spirits in the process.

We then see Saul cured via the use of a harp. Or as some commentaries point out, a natural cure to a seemingly supernatural disease. It is currently well known the power that music has on people. A common example that this illustration gets compared with is that of King Philip V. of Spain. He became so mentally unsound he could accomplish nothing. As a last-ditch effort, a famous musician named Farinelli was brought in. The music played by Farinelli caused King Philip to improve greatly and was back to normal in short order.

After all considerations, there is no conclusive evidence that would lead me to see this event as an example of demonic possession.

Then we come to the cases of Paul. The second situation of Paul is very unique, luckily almost all of the translations of this story are essentially identical.

We start in Acts 19:11-12 which states, "And God wrought special miracles by the hands of Paul: So that from his body were brought unto the sick handkerchiefs or aprons, and the diseases departed from them, and the evil spirits went out of them."

We are told that Paul through God was healing disease and eradicating "evil spirits." Unfortunately, there are no specific accounts of Paul's personal interactions with such spirits to be examined. Verses 13-16 then explain the following timeline of events,

"Then certain of the vagabond Jews, exorcists, took upon them to call over them which had evil spirits the name of the Lord Jesus, saying, We adjure you by Jesus whom Paul preacheth. And there were seven sons of one Sceva, a Jew, and chief of the priests, which did so. And the evil spirit answered and said, Jesus I know, and Paul I know; but who are ye? And the man in whom the evil spirit was leaped on them, and overcame them, and prevailed against them, so that they fled out of that house naked and wounded."

This one appears so cut and dry that few have taken the time read deeper into it. To begin with, the moral of the story has literally nothing to do with evil spirits or demons. The moral of the story is that those who attempt to use the word of God or the entity of God for personal gain will be punished. These "vagabond Jews" were essentially doing little more than a magic act, falsely claiming God, in order to profit. And so, they were punished.

In terms of the debate over whether or not the man involved was truly possessed or simply the victim of mental disease is, to me, much more difficult to determine in comparison to the case of Saul.

What does the "evil spirit" say or do that would indicate demonic possession but not mental illness.

Some may ignorantly claim that the knowledge of Jesus and Paul was supernatural knowledge, therefore demonic. This would only be true if we ignore verse 10 which states, "And this continued by the space of two years; so that all they which dwelt in Asia heard the word of the Lord Jesus, both Jews and Greeks." Knowledge of Jesus or Paul and what they stood for would have been common knowledge, not supernatural.

Then there is the argument of supernatural strength. The "seven sons." Having personally engaged people with mental illness, and even experienced their strength first hand, I have yet to encounter any mental illness that grants the type of strength that would be needed to not just escape from seven men, but to physically harm seven men to the degree espoused in the verse. Ultimately there is a limit to human strength even when mental illness is involved.

The pro-demonic argument here is that no mental illness could have allowed for such power, to overcome seven men. Which I would agree, except…

There is a known translation flaw with the verse where it states, "And the man in whom the evil spirit was leaped on them, and overcame them, and prevailed against them."

The use of the word "them," found in almost all current translations available today is misleading. The reader simply infers that "them" means "the seven sons."

Almost all of the exegetical commentaries point out this flaw including Meyer's NT, Expositors Greek Testament, the Cambridge Bible, and Bengal's Gnomen. The original Greek word used for *them* is **ἀμφοτέρων**. That word means *both*, not them. Or, only two of the seven sons are present during this account.

Could someone with severe mental health problems beat two men like this? That answer is certainly yes. Leaving us with no conclusive evidence of true demonic possession that cannot be equally explained by mental illness.

Though those who may wish to find demons everywhere in the bible might be unhappy with this conclusion, I actually find this verse as being extremely positive in terms of biblical validity.

In writing Acts 19, Luke has already introduced us to the "seven sons." Luke could have very easily manipulated or exaggerated this story to leave us believing that all seven were present and harmed by the demonic man, as would be expected in things such as mythological writing. This would have made the story even more powerful in terms of literary quality. However, Luke shows his intention toward accuracy by pointing out that in fact only two of them were present.

For me, the ability to defend the accuracy of the biblical accounts is far more relevant than whether or not the man involved was literally possessed by a demon or was just diseased in the mind.

Acts 16:17-18 provides our other example involving Paul.

"This girl followed Paul and the rest of us, shouting, "These men are servants of the Most High God, who are proclaiming to you the way of salvation." She continued this for many days. Eventually Paul grew so aggravated that he turned and said to the spirit, "In the name of Jesus Christ I command you to come out of her!" And the spirit left her at that very moment."

Though I agree to a certain extent with most commentaries that the girl involved here suffered from something, I struggle to find the implication of demonic possession. Possessed by something undoubtedly, but the word choice here by Luke does not seem to imply anything inherently evil. In all other used examples, the wording specifically reads "evil spirit" or "unclean spirit" yet here we are just given spirit (see: Luke 11:24,26). To conclude that this spirit was demonic leaves us only more confused to the nature of demon spirits. This young girl was correctly extolling Paul and Silas as servants of God.

Paul becomes annoyed with her as a distraction more than anything else and removes whatever it is that was plaguing her mind. There is often the argument that the girl's proclamation is an example of supernatural knowledge, but this seems again inaccurate and assumptive. Paul had not just showed up here, yet for some reason there is the inference made that no one knew who Paul was or what he was preaching. I struggle to find anything supernatural within this girl's proclamation that the average person could simply not have known.

The Gospels

Of the eight widely accepted accounts of possible demonic possession in the bible, five of the eight occur in the gospels of Matthew, Mark, and Luke. Very oddly, and for reasons I am not qualified to attest too, the Gospel of John mentions none of the five stories mentioned in the synoptic gospels. This is not particularly unique as John leaves out several other stories found in the synoptics, but it is worth pointing out.

A question often brought up is why Jesus appears to have so many interactions with demoniacs, the possessed, or evil spirits, whereas the rest of the bible provides scant examples of this.

The most common reason given for this by scholars is that the manifestation of God on Earth essentially leads to a counter increase in evil activity. Or to look at the argument from a Newtonian point of view, an action occurred and there was an opposing reaction. I have no logical quarrel with this explanation. However, I do think there are other possible explanations that are simpler and equally as likely.

One, Jesus was simply able to recognize possession or affliction more easily. Whereas the average person, even Paul, may not have the understanding, Jesus would have clearly known what was taking place. Or think of it this way: A doctor goes out into a town and diagnosis' many cases of cancer. A plumber goes out into the town and only diagnosis' one or two cases of cancer. Is this because there was less cancer or because one of the individuals was far more qualified to make such a diagnosis?

The second reason would be literary redundancy. Acts 19:12 "so that even handkerchiefs or aprons were brought from his body to the sick, and the diseases left them and the evil spirits went out of them."

The writers were clearly not concerned with documenting every single event that took place. Instead, we are provided just enough examples to show the power, without being inundated with the same examples over and over again. The gospels and Acts clearly indicate that there were many more accounts of such things happening, they simply do not mention them in detail.

Onto the accounts of Jesus, I choose to start with the story of the Canaanite woman. Matthew 15:22 states, "And a Canaanite woman from that region came to Him, crying out, "Lord, Son of David, have mercy on me! My daughter is miserably possessed by a demon."

We finally encounter a literal use of the word demon both in translation and the original language. **Δαιμονίζεται** (daimonizetai)

Izetai (possessed by)

Daimon (demon)

This story is very light on the details. We are told nothing about the characteristics of the daughter and the moral of the story is about faith, not demon possession. Jesus himself at no point references the daughter as being possessed by a demon or even an unclean spirit.

He simply tells the woman that her daughter has been healed.

Interestingly, in Mark's writing of the story, the woman is referenced as a Greek or Gentile. As the Pulpit Commentary elaborates on, the woman here was likely trying to word her statement to appeal to Jesus, as the gentiles did not believe that evil or demonic spirits caused any sort of malady, more so if we recall at this time the word *daemon* or *daimon* was not viewed as necessarily evil . The woman would have likely picked up the word meaning from the Hebrews in the area and was attempting to appeal to Jesus' religious sensibilities.

There is no definitive evidence in this story of demonic possession.

Matthew 17:18 "And Jesus rebuked the devil; and he departed out of him: and the child was cured from that very hour."

Here we find the word **δαιμόνιον** (daimonion). This passage is interesting in that it is prefaced by the reader being very specifically told that the boy involved had epilepsy.

What I enjoy is that this is the first passage we have come too that clearly shows an evil spirit or demon afflicting the child, yet it is also the only one so far that is clearly set-up first by a totally naturalistic explanation (epilepsy).

I do not accept coincidence that this story is written in this way. We are clearly given a biological explanation of the problem, only for us to be told... there is more to it than that. As if to say, sure it is biological, but then alludes to an underlying supernatural cause for the natural event to take place, that being some sort of evil or demonic force.

What I find to be even more interesting, is that today 2000 years later, the concept and disease of epilepsy is still very poorly understood. According to numerous research groups (i.e.

Citizens United for Research in Epilepsy, etc.) the cause of epilepsy is only known in a little under 50% of all cases. This means that in greater than 50% of all current epilepsy cases in the world, there is no known biological cause for the disease. I certainly see this story as the best so far for having a true biblical reference for demonic influence within a person that cannot be circumvented via purely a naturalistic explanation.

Matthew 12:22 (also Luke 11:14) "Then was brought unto him one possessed with a devil, blind, and dumb: and he healed him, insomuch that the blind and dumb both spake and saw."

This one simply left me confused. We encounter someone who is blind and mute and apparently possessed by a devil. Jesus heals him in short order. However, we are provided with no context as to the demon possessed elements. The implication is that the demon possession led to the physical ailments.

However, the story of Jesus healing the blind man in Mark 8 makes no similar connection. There is no reference to the blind man being possessed in any way. This begs the question of what was the difference between the two?

In reviewing the stories contextually, the biggest difference is audience. In the story of the demon possessed man, the Pharisees are found in attendance. They are not present when Jesus heals the blind man in Mark 8. Perhaps this was done for literary purposes, or perhaps it was based on the response by the audience. The Pharisees quickly condemn Jesus as acting under the power of "Beelzebul, prince of demons." It is arguable that the set-up of referring to him as possessed was more to drive home the later exchange. Though both sides have equal room for argumentation, I do not see this story as having the validity found in the story of the demon-possessed boy.

Mark 1:23-24 "Suddenly a man with an unclean spirit cried out in the synagogue: "What do You want with us, Jesus of Nazareth? Have You come to destroy us? I know who You are— the Holy One of God!"

The writers of the gospels certainly did not go out of their way to make this simple. Here was find the use of the term unclean spirit. Which leads to the question: "Why do the writers sometimes reference demons (*daimon*) specifically and yet other times use the phrase unclean or evil spirit?"

I have searched for a good answer as to why these literary

choices exist but have not found one that feels sufficient.

Several scholars make the presumption that evil/unclean spirits are specifically sent from God for punishment purposes. Whereas demons are essentially left to their own devices without such established purpose. No one explains how it is they reach this conclusion, so I generally am apprehensive to accept this point.

The issue of "unclean spirit" aside, we are left with what I consider the first actual case of supernatural knowledge, leading credence to this as being a valid case of demonic possession.

This is the first miracle performed by Jesus in the Book of Mark, and Jesus was essentially an unknown at this point. Yet, the man extols him to be "the Holy One of God." More revealing is the sentence, "Have you come to destroy us?"

Why would they assume such a thing? The idea that there is multiple voices, via the use of the word "us" is one thing. It might could even be chalked up to mental illness. But why would they assume Jesus was there to destroy them?

Matthew 8:28-29 "When Jesus arrived on the other side in the region of the Gadarenes, He was met by two demon-possessed men coming from the tombs. They were so violent that no one could pass that way. "What do You want with us, Son of God?" they shouted. "Have You come here to torture us before the appointed time?"

In this example we see a similar question posed by the one possessed. "Have you come to torture us?" Both of these examples provide strong evidence for truly supernatural knowledge. The idea being that these spirits felt that Jesus had already come to commence with a final judgement.

First, we ask the question of can we simply consider this mental illness related. I would objectively say no. I have personally spent thousands of hours around people who suffer from the most severe versions of mental illness known to man, everything from Bi-polar to schizophrenics and everything in between. I have never once entered the room or spoke to one of these people and they ask me if I have come to torture or destroy them, much less it be the very first thing they say to me.

The individuals of these accounts are speaking in regard to future events, that at the time were unknown. The idea that Jesus had come to "judge them before their time." I certainly believe both of these stories provide legitimate examples of demonic possession, primarily because this is what is claimed, and it is not easily washed away by claims of mental disease.

In total and excluding references to Satan, of the eight specific accounts regarding demonic possession in the bible, three of them appear to be legitimate to the extent that naturalistic explanations cannot be simply interceded in place of the supernatural.

C.S. Lewis once made the comment regarding the existence of demons, ""One is to disbelieve in their existence. The other is to believe, and to feel an excessive and unhealthy interest in them."

This is similar to other quotes made about Satan by other well-known scholars.

In all the accounts, including those that seem more open to interpretation, the ultimate outcome is that God was glorified. What leads to this glory is not particularly relevant in my opinion.

Satan and his demons exist for the same purpose that all other creatures exist for, to serve the purpose of and to glorify God.

Modern Day Demons

What happened to demons, evil spirits, and the like since the days of Christ? Did they finally surrender or give up?

This point is as, if not more, contentious than whether they ever existed to begin with.

To begin, in Catholicism the modern existence of demons or evil spirits is not a traditionally debated topic. Catholicism has always held to the existence of demons or evil spirits, even to this day. Many people think that the use of exorcism is something only popularized by movies and that

Catholicism does not actually believe or practice this.

Consider this, several studies of varying scientific validity have found that the use of Catholic exorcism is increasing in the U.S. over the past few decades. The *Catechisms of the Catholic Church* authored in 1992 by Pope John Paul II reaffirms the Catholic belief in exorcism. In 1999 the Catholic Church revised a document called *Of Exorcisms and Certain Supplications*, an 84-page document listing in details the approved ritual format for exorcism. There is also the *Rituale Romanum* which describes in exact detail the approved process for performing exorcisms.

Official guidelines for Catholic exorcism's can be traced back to 1614. Prior to this canonizing of guidelines, Priest would use differing guidelines or simply make up their own. However, there is complete historical evidence that Catholic exorcism has existed since its founding and has never fallen out of favor. A lot of this evidence is found via ancient artwork depicting exorcisms such as the *Exorcism of St. Benedict* painted in 1387.

But what about the protestant view? Whereas Catholics are bound to fall-in line, protestant

Christianity runs the gambit on beliefs. In modern liberal theology, Satan and demons are non-existent. They are simply explanatory representations for the natural evil of humans. However, conservative theology rejects this claim as being plainly anti-doctrinal and anti-Christian, bordering on outright heresy.

Martin Luther essentially had no independent opinion on the topic, as he held to the traditional Catholic beliefs regarding demons and evil spirits.

John Calvin on the other hand had very, very strong opinions on the subject, which to be objective sometimes appear to have more to do with his hatred toward Catholicism than anything else.

In Calvin's *Institutes of Christian Religion,* we find in Book IV that Calvin certainly believed in demonic or evil spirits. In Chapter 19 Calvin writes, "Scarcely will you find one in ten who is not possessed by a wicked spirit."

Not just a believer in the spirits of evil, but Calvin believed that a far higher percentage than what we may think are under the influence of these wicked spirits. However, Calvin was likely making this point to further disparage the Catholic Church and their practices.

John Wesley appears to have taken a much more literal view. In the mid 1700's, Wesley documents in his journals numerous accounts of his interactions with people appearing to be possessed by demons or evil spirits.

As we move forward into the 1800's, we begin to see a slight shift in the view of demon possession. There is no way to truly know how much or to what extent these conservative theologians were being influenced by the new breed of liberal theology, but to some extent a shift in thinking was taking place.

On June 10th of 1883 famous theologian Charles Spurgeon gave a sermon which included this statement,

"I suppose that we have never seen Satanic possession, although I am not quite sure about it; for some men exhibit symptoms which are very like it. The present existence of demons within the bodies of men I shall neither assert nor deny; but certainly, in our Savior's day it was very common for devils to take possession of men and torment them greatly. It would seem that Satan was let loose while Christ was here below that the serpent might come into personal conflict with the appointed seed..."

Here we see Spurgeon assert a more modern response. Maybe or maybe not, it simply was not for him to decide or know. He also makes the argument for greater demonic presence during the time of Christ.

This view would become the overwhelming popularized belief moving into the 20th century and generally echoed by the likes of Karl Barth and C.S. Lewis. The opinion as a bare bones concept being: Satan certainly exists as does his demons. They likely still influence the minds of people, particularly the unbeliever. But the extent to which they intervene in the lives of men, and certainly in regard to direct demonic possession, can simply not be known concretely.

This "Spurgeonesque" view is very similar to a Calvinistic view. Calvin believed that these evil forces still had a great impact on the modern world, but equally threw it into a category of those things which are not meant to be known.

In his rage against the Catholic Church, Calvin used this belief structure to question the priestly hierarchies. Calvin, in his traditionally hyper-rationalistic way, made the point that if Catholic Priest could cast out demons or evil spirits through some dogmatic prayer or chant, why did they simply not drive out all the forces of evil found on the Earth and cleanse the world of all the evil spirits?

It was not that Calvin disbelieved in the existence, he disbelieved that some modern priest could have the same biblical power's possessed by Jesus or the apostles. In the story of the demon possessed boy, verse 19 states, "Afterward the disciples came to Jesus privately and asked, "Why couldn't we drive it out?"

Calvin's view is that there were cases where even Jesus' own disciples were incapable of such a task, yet a Catholic priest reciting a pre-planned prayer would somehow rise to the level of faith needed to drive out similar entities, greater than the faith of Jesus' own disciples?

In this comparison we see two different trains of thoughts: the well-intentioned emotionally driven ideology of the Catholic Church compared to the purely rationalistic thinking of traditional conservative protestant theology.

In other world religions we also find the modern belief in demonism and evil spirits. Islam, Hinduism, and numerous African tribal religions all firmly believe in the modern presence of evil spirits. Hinduism, as one example, still commonly blame things even as basic as relationship problems on the presence of the *boori atma* or evil spirit.

In other realms of supernatural belief there is a lot of unknowns. People, especially in Western cultures, often wrongfully associate Occult practices with the belief in demons. This is incorrect in that Occult is purely subjective to the individual belief structure, in which the person simply chooses whatever they want to believe. Yes, often things such as Jewish Mysticism are labeled "occultic." But this is not a one size fits all label. For instance, someone who believes that meditation will bring them higher enlightenment, could equally be labeled occultic without ever having to believe in demons or evil spirits.

Another group are those who belong to the "Wiccan" (Wicca) movement. Or, the modernized name for witchcraft. These individual's entire belief structure is based on two things, the existence of supernatural spirits and worship of the natural world.

Wiccans practice ritual sacrifice, prayer, and necromancy. They firmly believe in being able to communicate with dead or other supernatural spirits. Wicca itself is not an ancient religion, the term itself does not even spring up until the 1950's. However, it is based on ancient pagan religions and practices. Though they do not believe in one God or one Devil, they certainly believe in many different God's and devils. In case you think this is some weird extremist group that doesn't really exist, the U.S. government estimates that approximately 400,000 Americans actively practice Wicca as their religion. That is just in the U.S. and does not include other groups who engage in witchcraft that do not claim Wicca as a religion.

We also come to the topic of *Satanism*. The actual worship of Satan. This is actually a modern invention, not an ancient one. Often this whole topic is thought of as little more than ancient folklore that no educated modern man or woman would subscribe to. Yet oddly, the literal Church of Satan was not founded until 1966. So as much as some would like to believe this is some ancient problem, it is very modern in many respects.

The history of Satanism is extremely complicated. As Christianity expanded to new countries, just about every pagan religion encountered was essentially considered Satanist since it worshipped false gods. This seeming misuse of the term Satanist was used up until the mid-

1800's when the naturalist movement, led in large part by the works of Darwin, revitalized and gave new meaning to the term.

Stanislaw Przybyszewski was one of the original thinkers behind the idea of "nature worship" drawing heavily on the works of Darwin. Essentially, if we no longer have a God to worship, then we worship nature.

I would be remiss not to bring up Romans 1:25 where Paul wrote this famous verse, "They exchanged the truth of God for a lie, and worshiped and served the creature rather than the Creator, who is forever worthy of praise! Amen."

Well needless to say, Paul correctly predicted this one for certain. The nature worship mentality would evolve into modern Satanism by the mid 1900's.

There is two modern forms of Satanism; there is theistic Satanism and atheistic Satanism. Theistic Satan worship views Satan and demons as actual beings to be worshipped. They believe in a type of pure dualism. That Satan is directly opposite but equally as powerful as God. Atheistic Satanism, such is the modern view held by the Church of Satan, simply believes in nature worship though not in the traditional sense.

They believe people should quite literally be allowed to do anything they want and that all those moral rules put in place by the Abrahamic religions are horrible.

No one knows how many people belong to these groups because they intentionally refuse to release their numbers.

Slightly off-topic, but there is a very humorous article written a few years ago by CNN that openly defends and, in many ways, applauds the Church of Satan. It also claims wrongly that the Church of Satan never actually worshipped Satan, though it is well documented that upon its founding Anton LaVey (the literal founder) had a church in San Francisco and would gather for "unknown" rituals. CNN just calls them fun freedom loving libertarians…

Other groups such as the Temple Set also exist and openly take to theistic Satanism where they quite literally worship Satan.

Post-Biblical Examinations

If we recall in Catholicism, there is still a large segment of the Christian Church along with other world religions and groups, who firmly believe demonic possession still occurs from time to time. For the purposes of removing the easy explanation of "they simply did not understand medical diagnoses," we will look at some examples which have occurred since 1750.

It should be understood that there is numerous accounts of demonic possession running through every century. For brevity, we will jump forward to the point in time where medical advancement was really taking off.

Since this time, even in just cursory research, there has been easily over 50 documented reports of demonic possession just in Western Europe and North America. The actual documented number of cases could likely be far higher. So, the question remains, are even these modern examples little more than attempts to explain the medically unknown. Another reason for choosing a starting date of 1750 is that the enlightenment was well underway by this point, and skepticism abounded.

One of the more famous European cases occurs in 1788 and involved 44-year-old George Lukins. This account was heavily documented and even written about in the heavily read *Bristol Gazette*.

According to records and Lukins own accounts, he became "demon possessed" around the age of 26. Lukins had been performing in a Christmas pageant when, as he claims, he originally became possessed. From that point on, Lukins suffered from an array of strange behaviors. He would scream randomly and in different voices, could become highly violent, and made odd barking noises. He would occasionally makes claims of being the devil and would sing the classic Latin hymn *Te Deum* inverted. All of these different behaviors were documented heavily, including in local newspapers.

Lukins had been seen by numerous physicians during this time period, including Dr. Smith of Wrington, one of the top regional surgeons of the period. Lukins was eventually declared incurable. In 1788, an exorcism led by Reverend Joseph Easterbrook along with several other ministers, appears to have cured Lukins. It is reported that he lived out the rest of his life normal, calm, and happy after the exorcism.

As accounts swirled around Western Europe, there was a great deal of interest in this case. With skepticism so high, numerous people posited arguments against Lukins and his exorcism.

One argument was that Lukins suffered from epilepsy. This was a bad argument in that it only would have accounted for a very specific behavior, not all of Lukins behaviors. It also basically claims that all of the doctors Lukins visited were not smart enough to diagnose the problem as being epilepsy. Considering the medical beginnings of epilepsy date back to roughly 400 B.C., any half-trained doctor would have likely been able to diagnose the problem.

Another claim is that Lukins was a trained actor, even a

ventriloquist, and that this whole ordeal was little more than a charade.

From the apologetics perspective, we often find this argument, which mostly amounts to circular reasoning and revisionist history anytime the natural and supernatural seem to bump heads.

What we find is basically atheistic faith appearing. There is no supernatural, so I put my faith purely in the natural, even if there is no evidence for the natural in this case. There is zero documentation of Lukins being a trained actor, much less a trained ventriloquist. All documentation from the actual time period points out that Lukins was a common tailor. The assertion is made that because one-time Lukins appeared in his towns Christmas pageant that he was somehow a classically trained actor. This would be like me appearing in my middle school play on the Gettysburg Address and then twenty years later someone claiming I was an official "actor" because of my role. The claim continues that Lukins was simply "acting" demon possessed, for 18 years! Not exactly scientific arguments.

Currently, there is several mental health disorders which discuss delusions, such as being the devil. It is most typically associated with the mania cycle in Bi-polar disorder. I have personally encountered people who thought they were Jesus or an angel. Though it is far rarer, thinking you were the devil would also fall into this mental health category. The issue of different voices would likely be characterized under Schizophrenia.

However, the apparent sudden onset of all these illnesses simultaneously and the sudden relief from all these illnesses simultaneously, is not something the mental health or medical community can scientifically account for with any validity.

The next example I bring up only because some have argued that there have been no accounts of possible demonic possession in Great Britain since the Lukins case in the 1700's. Again, naturalist want to minimize the supernatural at all points, so claiming, "Ha-ha see, since the enlightenment ended, no demons in Britain."

A very famous case from 1974 that is still heavily discussed today involved Michael Taylor. A man who went through an exorcism after claiming he felt a great evil within him.

Father Peter Vincent led a two-day exorcism with Taylor. In the aftermath, the clergy had claimed to have removed as many as forty demons from Taylor but claimed that at least some remained within him. To be very clear, this seems highly revisionist on the part of the priest involved.

At the end of the exorcist event, Taylor was sent home. He then proceeded that same day to brutally murder his wife with his bare hands. This included gauging her eyes completely out, ripping her tongue out, and literally trying to tear her face off. He then strangled their Poodle to death, went out into the street naked, and passed out. Where he was then found by the police.

He then spent the rest of his life in the combination of prisons and psychiatric hospitals. Interestingly enough, the psychiatric facilities had no idea what was wrong with Taylor other than to say he suffered from "psychosis."

There exist far more cases ranging from Germany to North America to South Africa. Famous cases such Roland Doe, to which the book *The Exorcist* was written on. The cases of Anneliese Michel and Clara Germana Cele to name a few specific examples.

Many of the cases fall under the problem of minimal documentation. For instance, the

Clara Cele case was well documented, but only by the nun and priest which attended to her.

The famous Roland Doe case had as many as forty-nine separate witnesses, but critics claim that none of those forty-nine did a successful job in analyzing all of the evidence.

In review of these cases, there is two main arguments made against the claim of demonic possession... mental illness and "it was all a big prank."

We are going to ignore the "it was all a prank" critic. There is a surprising number of critics who chalk many of these cases up to being a hoax. The idea that a 13-year-old boy would undergo numerous exorcisms and subject himself to extreme physical and psychological stress to that degree just for some attention seems at least a little bit intellectually lazy. Or that someone would pretend to be demon possessed for 18-years just to have a good laugh seems to border on absurd. These claims are rarely supported by evidence of their assertions.

Instead we fall back to the age-old question, is it all just mental illness mis understood?

Failure of Psychology

Increasingly, even Christians are throwing the ideas of demon possession under the umbrella of mental illness. It is after all much more scientific and makes you sound less crazy. When I was working in clinical settings, surrounded by those with Schizophrenia and Bi-polar, I was shocked to see just how tormented some of these human brains had become. But I could not shake the question of "how."

The field of psychology, in large part thanks to the efforts of organizations such as the American Psychological Association, has convinced the general public that they have an extremely thorough understanding of mental illness while truthfully having minimal to no idea what it is they are talking about.

Not to take everything away from the field, they have gained an amazing amount of insight into our animal brains. The Limbic System in our brains, which includes the amygdala, hypothalamus, and hippocampus, controls our emotions. Special attention has been given to the amygdala, which helps control our emotional response to the environment and events surrounding us.

Psychology and the medical field in general have gained quite a bit of understanding into how this region works and impacts us. This is in part because it is universal. Almost every mammal on Earth has this same region in their brain. Therefore, scientist and psychologist have been able to study animals to better understand how the region works in our own minds. Have you ever known a dog that seemingly gets anxious when it's owner leaves? The same region of the brain that controls our feelings of anxiety is identical to that of the dog.

For this reason, purely emotional based issues such as anxiety and depression are far easier to understand in terms of "why" and "how."

But what of those mental diseases that we claim are behind demonic possession? Primarily, Schizophrenia, Bi-polar disorder, Dissociative Identity Disorder, and of course epilepsy (?) which we have already briefly discussed that science only has a partial understanding of.

Let us see what the experts have to say here:

According to the Mayo Clinic: "It's not known what causes schizophrenia."

According to the Mayo Clinic: "The exact cause of bipolar disorder is unknown."

For Dissociative Identity Disorder (DID), the claim is that childhood trauma causes it almost universally. But honestly, they have no clue. Take this excerpt from the *California Institute of Behavioral Neurosciences and Psychology*:

All of these regions are *somehow* affected in the DID patient's brain...

Why the nature of these symptoms is temporary despite evidence for permanent structural brain changes is perhaps a question that is yet to be answered.

Perhaps... So, let me break this down for everyone into easy logical terms... Someone experiences *trauma*, which in the world of psychology basically means anything you do not enjoy... it then causes a "permanent structural change in the brain," but... this only results in symptoms which kind of just show up whenever they feel like it.

Basically, we do not know, we do not know, and then we are pretty sure we know but it makes zero sense logically.

The claim is: let us say your mother died when you were 10 and this was very traumatic for you (understandable). The claim is that somehow this event will literally interrupt the biological development of your brain through some (pun intended) supernatural occurrence, but then after your brain permanently transforms it only impacts you randomly, and only once you reach adulthood (children do not get diagnosed with DID).... It is quite literally junk science at its finest, in which we are required to make enormous leaps of faith (which is fine as long as it's a naturalistic faith of course).

Here is some other fine examples of faith put forward from the field of psychology:

From ScienceDirect: "Pope *et al.* (2007) suggested that dissociative amnesia (or DID) is a contemporary culture-bound syndrome and offered a reward of US$1000 "to the first individual who could find a case of dissociative amnesia for a traumatic event in any fictional or non-fictional work before 1800" (p. 225)."

Here they are basically saying this whole idea is made up. Or think of it this way… for thousands of years kids lived highly traumatic lives, just think about the mortality rates for children. Yet, there is not a single piece of evidence in all of history for this current disease. It is little more than a culturally made-up disease to provide adults with excuses for bad or irregular behavior because "life is hard."

Healthline on Schizophrenia: "researchers don't completely understand what causes schizophrenia…. chemicals are *believed* to play a role."

Mayo Clinic: "researchers *believe* that…"

National Health System UK: "The exact cause of bipolar disorder is unknown. Experts *believe*…"

If you wish to play a fun game, look up any of these diseases and select an article at random. Then, count how many times the word "may," "believe," "suggests," or "probably," is used.

The truth is that even with all the medical advancement of the last century, what causes these "demonic" like behaviors is still far from understood. However, it is perfectly okay to "believe" in these diseases. Faith and belief is preferred only when talking about the natural world apparently.

The argument that demonic possession is no more than an explanation for mental illness would be great if we actually understood mental illness. In fairness, to do this switch we are doing little more than taking one thing we do not understand and replacing it with something else that we do not understand, purely for the sake of naturalism and "science."

Does this mean every account of demonic possession should simply be accepted? Of course not. But we equally cannot write off every case via mental illness, primarily due to the fact that we do not really understand what mental illness is to begin with.

To further this point, look at the efficacy (success) rates of medications for mental illness. Even for the supposedly best understood diseases (such as depression) the efficacy rates of the most commonly prescribed medicines sit only between 15-25%. So, these mind-altering medicines only work on about 2/10 people, and this is without factoring in the horrific and sometimes deadly side effects of these medicines.

On top of this you have to understand, there is not a single cure for any "mental illness." Not. A. Single. One. Not for depression, not for anxiety, not for Schizophrenia. All of those medicines are designed to "lessen" your symptoms. They are a mask that (about 20% of the time) covers up the problem. Most of the time, this is done strictly via tranquilizing effects. So, your symptoms go away but your life is still miserable because you do not even feel like doing anything. You get "zombified," so to speak.

If you think I am simply being harsh on the field of psychology to win a religious argument... Consider that in 2008 a famous psychiatrist named Thomas Szasz wrote an entire book called *Psychiatry: The Science of Lies*. A man with a Ph.D. in the field literally abhorred what an abject failure the field had become.

Most of this stems from money of course. People have problems, we simply had to figure out a way to monetize that problem. Look at how much money the pharmaceutical industry makes off of their pills with a 20% efficacy rate (hint: it is in the 10's of billions annually).

With all that said, I certainly believe people suffer from torments of the mind. And I also certainly would argue that some of these issues I have encountered personally are in fact the results of certain traumas, genetic, or other biological factors. However, I would also say these are exceptions, not the rule.

In our quest to rid this realm of the supernatural, we have capitalized on human misery.

Turned to pseudoscience to replace the supernatural. And from a certain standpoint sacrificed the human to rid ourselves of God.

There may be certain instances where mental illness is a fitting alternative to the claim of demonic possession, but it is far from an all-inclusive alternative.

A Doctrinal Approach

We arrive at the question, after analyzing the evidence surrounding what is currently understood; what is or should be the Christian stance toward the topic of demonic possession? Specifically, when it comes to the defense of scriptures.

The very first and most critical point of all of this, is that the concept or belief in demon possession is not a necessary pillar of the Christian faith. Essentially, other than in defense of the infallibility of the Holy Bible, the issue of demonic possession is irrelevant. If every story alluding to demonic possession was removed from the Bible, it would change nothing in regard to the core beliefs all Christians must share.

Salvation by grace through faith, the incarnation, death, resurrection, ascension, and eventual return of Jesus Christ; these stories cannot be replaced and are the backbone for the Christian religion.

However, we still must address the issue of infallibility. In most Christian denominations, this is considered a core belief. Often times, this is discussed via the lens of being the perfect and inspired direct word of God given to man.

There is a host of possible takes on this and it has become even more skewed in the last 200 years with the rise in liberal theology.

To start with the most basic point, a Christian must believe in the existence of demons or evil spirits. Far too many Christians fall into the "bed of roses" trap with this issue. I personally have known too many people who say they believe in God, Jesus, and angels (all the happy and good things right); but they will simply turn right around and claim they do not believe in Satan or demons. This is not a biblically sound approach, is destructive to all other apologetic arguments, and fails to follow any sort of basic logical structure.

As Dr. Sproul pointed out, why would you believe in one but not the other? If you believe in God or angels, you already believe in the supernatural. Yet, many Christians feel some sort of weird embarrassment when it comes to claiming Satan or other evil entities. How can you feel reasonable in defending the one but not the other? They both equally fall under the category of supernatural concepts that cannot be quantified or qualified by modern scientific standards.

A side note to that, if anything is self-evident within our

current world, it should be that evil forces exist. Simply look around you. To the Christian, it should actually be easier to argue for the existence of evil, more so than the idea of some sacred good in many instances. The evil has become so much easier to see.

It is also dangerous to take the liberalized approach, or the approach of many Jewish sects, and to claim that the references to Satan or demons is just an explanatory way of addressing the evil nature of humans. The reason for this is that it likewise damages other apologetic related arguments.

If I were to take the atheistic position, I would simply ask that person, "So, is the concept of God, Jesus, and angels simply an adverse metaphor for the good nature of humans?" To which they would then reply to the contrary, thus creating a self-defeating and illogical position. There is not a scriptural basis for the claim that the use of Satan, demons, or evil spirits was meant to simply be a literary tool describing the evil by nature state of humans. Out of the 66 canonized protestant books, you would have to assume at least one would have mentioned such an enormous idea, even if just in a passing verse. But it is not to be found. In our attempts to create some sort of "better" bible, we have added concepts or thought processes to the writers that they never actually wrote themselves. Our attempts to do this are no more than trying to revise what the bible says in order to make it easier for *US* to understand.

In terms of defending the actual stories themselves regarding demonic possession, I see no major issue for the Christian. First, each story must be taken as a unique account and approached as such. There is no reason trying to beat your head against a wall when it is not needed. The story of Saul is easily attributable to depression or the "spirit of sadness." To start with, do not defend demons that do not exist. There is no conclusive evidence in the scripture that alludes to Saul ever actually being possessed by a "demon."

Another point to be brought up as a possible defense is that it is simply impossible to know exactly what is the message, or, what did the author mean. Some might say this is a cop-out argument, but that makes it no less valid of a point.

How much has the English language changed just in the time you have been alive, specifically in regard to the way we speak and write it? For me it has changed quite a bit. Now, imagine how much languages have changed over the last 2,000 years. Now imagine we are trying to translate one language into other languages over that same enormous period of time. Consider this, there is currently 10's of thousands of words in other languages that there is no direct translation for into English. And this is just within languages that are loosely based off of ancient Latin and Greek. When we move into Asian languages, we have a whole different issue in translation. It raises the age-old question: The Bible as the word of God is infallible, but humans less so.

This is why in many of these accounts, acting as though you know exactly what was written, how it was written, and how it was meant to be received is a fool's errand. This is not a "get out of jail free card." It is simply meant as a warning against defending something from a point of ignorance. Unless you have really dug into the older or more direct translations surrounding these verses, you are likely better off admitting to ignorance and moving along.

In terms of defending the accounts that certainly may require defense, such as those involving Jesus himself, these are not particularly difficult to defend. This is because the counter argument is equally indefensible, at least at this point in time. What was it that possessed these people? As soon as the mental illness argument is made, the argument ends. You can simply ask, "Which mental illness?" They may tell you one, at which point you simply ask, "What causes that mental illness?" At which point they either make up a cause that has not been proven (arguing from ignorance) or admit they do not know what causes it, which means they are just as unknowing of the exact nature of it as you are.

The other argument which those who are more comfortable

simply arguing miracles in general could make is, "okay so what if it was mental illness?" Even if the other person was right, does it diminish from the supernatural power? How many people have you met who can simply speak a single sentence to a mentally ill person and immediately cure it? I have yet to meet one with such an ability.

I have had the unfortunate position of being the first person to arrive to reports of suicide. I have been to and seen up close, at this point, more than thirty people who have committed suicide. Hanging, poisoning, the self-inflicted gunshot wound...

I was at one once, and another guy was with me who was at a minimum agnostic in his belief system. The person, now deceased, had taken a .40 caliber handgun, placed it to their chest, and pulled the trigger.

I asked my partner at the scene, "What do you think drives a person to such an act?" To which he replied, "Something has to simply eat at your soul, to the point your soul has already died."

I did not disagree with him at all but was slightly shocked by his answer. Whether or not demonic possession takes place to the extent it was written about in the Bible, I do not claim to know. But I would argue until I was blue in the face that there is something evil that exist in our world. It is not sufficient enough an answer to see someone with a hole going through their brain and say, "I guess they had a mental illness." It is a totally inadequate explanation.

There is, in my experience, certainly a force; call it demons, evil spirits, or whatever you may like, that breaks a person down in a way that biology does not have an answer for. For that reason, I see no illegitimacy in claiming demons as real entities.

The evil forces that be, are all around us, but we simply ignore them or are too blind to see them. If all evil, all human pain and misery, is simply explained through biological forces... then why is so much evil, pain, and suffering so unique to humans?

I will relinquish my claim to evil spirits the day my cat or dog commits suicide. If all evil influence is simple brain biology, I would suspect the first case to be any day now.

"O the depth of the riches both of the wisdom and knowledge of God! How unsearchable are his judgments, and his ways past finding out!

For who hath known the mind of the Lord? or who hath been his counsellor?

Or who hath first given to him, and it shall be recompensed unto him again?

For of him, and through him, and to him, are all things: to whom be glory for ever. Amen."

About the Author

Stephen Hancock was born and raised in metro-Atlanta, Georgia. He currently lives in Alabama with his wife and three children.

Stephen has approximately seven years working in the field of law enforcement where has routinely encountered the mentally ill. He has also worked in local mental health clinics and has had extensive interaction working with those diagnosed with Schizophrenia, Bi-Polar Disorder, Adult Autism, and other mental health disorders.

Stephen has a Bachelor's of Science Degree from Southern New Hampshire University and a Master's Degree in Psychology from Amridge Christian University.

This author can be reached at:

Jcastrowritings2020@gmail.com

9 7 9 8 6 8 3 4 5 0 9 1 5